DATE DUE

Chandra, Deborah.

Miss Mabel's table.

MISS MABEL'S TABLE

MISS MABEL'S TABLE

Written by Deborah Chandra

ILLUSTRATED BY MAX GROVER

BROWNDEER PRESS
HARCOURT BRACE & COMPANY
San Diego New York London

Requests for permission to make copies of
any part of the work should be mailed to:
Permissions Department,
Harcourt Brace & Company,
8th Floor, Orlando, Florida 32887.

Library of Congress Cataloging-in-Publication Data
Chandra, Deborah.
Miss Mabel's table/by Deborah Chandra;
pictures by Max Grover.
—1st ed.
p. cm.
"Browndeer Press."
Summary: A cumulative counting rhyme presents
the ingredients and techniques used by Miss Mabel
to cook enough pancakes to serve ten people.
ISBN 0-15-276712-6
[1. Pancakes, waffles, etc.—Fiction.
2. Cookery—Fiction. 3. Counting.
4. Stories in rhyme.]
I. Grover, Max, ill. II. Title.
PZ8.3.C363Mi 1994
[E]—dc20 93-9137

First edition
A B C D E

Printed in Singapore

To Nathan and to Sam,
for all the times
we've counted to ten
—D. C.

For all my friends, old and new
—M. G.

This is Miss Mabel's table.

This is one frying pan, big and bold,
waiting to cook on the kitchen stove,
but now, so quiet and empty and cold,
sits on Miss Mabel's table.

COOK BOOK

These are two teaspoons heaped with salt,
that lie near the frying pan, big and bold,
waiting to cook on the kitchen stove,
but now, so quiet and empty and cold,
sits on Miss Mabel's table.

KITTY
CHOW

These are the glasses, one, two, three,
brimming with milk, that quietly
stand near the teaspoons, one and two,
that lie near the frying pan, big and bold,
waiting to cook on the kitchen stove,
but now, so quiet and empty and cold,
sits on Miss Mabel's table.

Four cups of flour—one, two, three, four
(carefully measured, not less, not more),
rest near five eggs, smooth and white,
that calmly wait in the morning light
that shines on the glasses, one, two, three,
brimming with milk that quietly
stand near the teaspoons, one and two,
that lie near the frying pan, big and bold,
waiting to cook on the kitchen stove,
but now, so quiet and empty and cold,
sits on Miss Mabel's table.

Six pinches of cinnamon, freshly ground,
and seven sweet strawberries, ripe and round,
pile in a dish in the morning light,
that shines on five eggs, smooth and white,
that wait near the flour (four cups, no more),
by the glasses of milk—one, two, three,
standing together quietly,
near teaspoons of salt—here's one and two,
that lie near the frying pan, big and bold,
waiting to cook on the kitchen stove,
but now, so quiet and empty and cold,
sits on Miss Mabel's table.

Eight pats of butter, yellow and soft,
melt in a platter right next to the spot
where seven sweet strawberries, ripe and round,
with six pinches of cinnamon, freshly ground,
pile in a dish in the morning light
that shines on five eggs, smooth and white,
that wait near the flour (four cups, no more),
by the glasses of milk—one, two, three,
standing together quietly,
near teaspoons of salt—here's one and two,
that lie near the frying pan, big and bold,
waiting to cook on the kitchen stove,
but now, so quiet and empty and cold,
sits on Miss Mabel's table.

NEWS

Nine spoons of sugar glisten like snow—
six, seven, eight, nine, straight in a row,
near eight pats of butter, yellow and soft,
that melt in a platter right next to the spot
where seven sweet strawberries, ripe and round,
with six pinches of cinnamon, freshly ground,
pile in a dish in the morning light
that shines on five eggs, smooth and white,
that wait near the flour (four cups, no more)
by glasses of milk—one, two, three,
standing together quietly,
by teaspoons of salt—here's one and two,
that lie near the frying pan, big and bold,
waiting to cook on the kitchen stove,
but now, so quiet and empty and cold,
sits on Miss Mabel's table.

CLOSED

This, to the side, is a tiny tin plate,
where ten dashes of yeast so peacefully wait,
where all things are silent and restful and still,
where only the sun moves its warm light that spills
over glasses and spoons and the dishes that fill
all of Miss Mabel's table.
Where nine spoons of sugar glisten like snow—
six, seven, eight, nine, straight in a row,
near eight pats of butter, yellow and soft,
that melt in a platter right next to the spot
where seven sweet strawberries, ripe and round,

with six pinches of cinnamon, freshly ground,
pile in a dish in the morning light
that shines on five eggs, smooth and white,
that wait near the flour (four cups, no more),
by the glasses of milk—one, two, three,
standing together quietly,
by teaspoons of salt—here's one and two,
that lie near the frying pan, big and bold,
waiting to cook on the kitchen stove,
but now, so quiet and empty and cold,
sits on Miss Mabel's table.

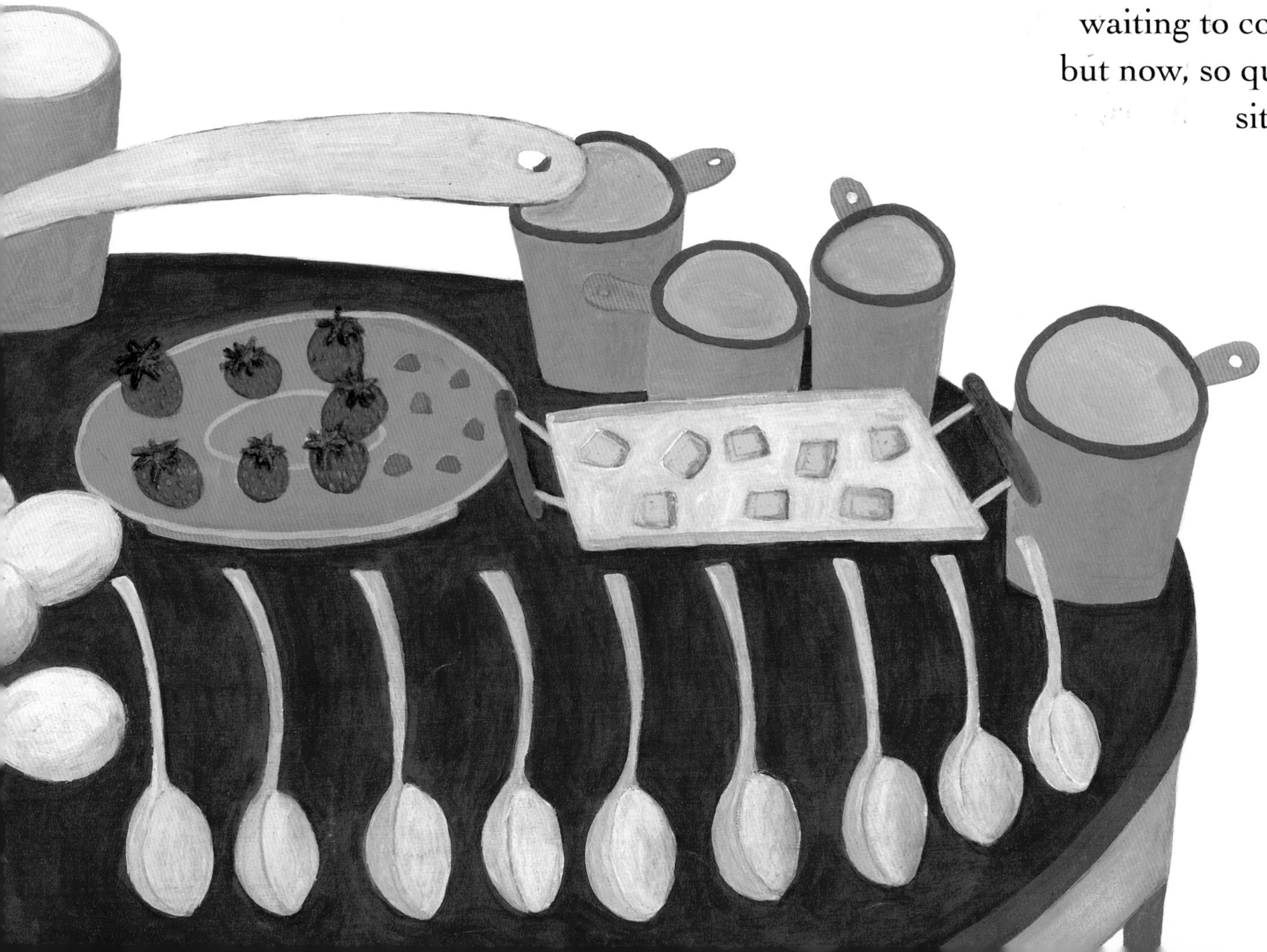

Suddenly, someone begins to scrape
ten dashes of yeast off the tiny tin plate,
beating them round in a big blue bowl
with nine spoons of sugar that glisten like snow.
Stirring, she adds with a hollow *plop*
eight pats of butter, yellow and soft,
and seven sweet strawberries, ripe and round,
with six pinches of cinnamon, freshly ground.

CLOSED
ANO
VERS

Then quickly cracks five eggs, smooth and white,
that slide down the bowl in the morning light.
Faster and faster she stirs as she pours
four cups of flour (not less, not more),
with a clatter and splash she adds noisily
the glasses of milk—blending one, two, three.
Now it's all that a churn of her strong arm can do
to stir in the teaspoons of salt—one and two.

ABEL'S
BLE

Tipping the bowl with a steady hand,
she pours out the mix in the frying pan
that's big and bold and cooks on the stove,
full of batter that bubbles and spatters
with berries and flour growing bigger and browner,
it simmers and sputters with sugar and butter,
it sizzles and makes
hot, golden pancakes—
all for Miss Mabel's table.

Who is this someone who stirs the big bowl,
and licking her fingers, now cooks at the stove,
who is going to eat as soon as she's able
hot pancakes with syrup?
It's hungry Miss Mabel!

How many people will she feed then?

One, two, three, four, five, six, seven, eight, nine, ten!

Right here, at her very own table.

The paintings in this book were done in acrylics
on D'Arches Lavis Fedelis drawing paper.
The text type was set in Cochin.
The display type was set in Greco Deco,
portions of which were hand-lettered
by the illustrator.
Composition by Harcourt Brace & Company
Photocomposition Center, San Diego, California.
Color separations by Bright Arts, Ltd., Singapore
Printed and bound by Tien Wah Press, Singapore
Production supervision by Warren Wallerstein
and David Hough
Designed by Michael Farmer